Post-Apocalyptic Joe in a Cinematic Wasteland

Episode One: When It Rains, It Pours

Joe Gillis

SLACKER ENTERTAINMENT BOOKS are published by Jowagi Productions

Edited by Rachel Gillis

Cover art by Joe Gillis

ISBN: 978-1-963072-00-6

Digital edition: ISBN: 978-1-963072-01-3 (e-book)

Download Free Audiobook

Thank you for purchasing the print version. As a bonus, I'm throwing in the audiobook version of this book for free.

Download at **joegillis.com/audiobook1**

EPISODE ONE
WHEN IT RAINS, IT POURS

CHAPTER 1

The mushroom-shaped cloud enveloped the sky, emitting a fiery glow of pure fury as the billowing mass of anger ripped across the surface. The light was so intense that it felt as though it was burning my eyes. The blinding intensity made me thankful I had decided to wear my vintage aviator goggles, which were tinted for such occasions—well, not for end of the world horribleness, but you know, very bright occasions. So I went ahead and I pulled them down from my forehead over my eyes, which allowed me to continue to watch. It was the most devastating thing I had ever seen—yet it was strangely peaceful at the same time. Of course, it might have helped that I was standing on a bridge far outside its destructive reach. The longer I stood there, the more it burned my eyes. Lifting my arm up, I was able to shield my eyes enough to continue to bask in its beauty. I watched in awe as it grew larger and larger. Part of the calmness was probably the fact that the explosion seemed to suck in all audible noise before expelling it all back out as a tremendous BOOM. Then, a huge gust of wind and intense heat blew over me as the shockwave struck my body head-on, lifting my hair into a wild dance behind me. Gripping the handrail in front of me tightly, I planted my feet firmly so I wouldn't get swept away by the strong gale-force winds. My clothes felt as though something was trying to wrench them from my body as gusts of wind shook me from side to side. Without warning, a giant tidal wave surged from the nearby river, raging like a hurricane before drenching me in its wake.

The water was loosening my grip on both the ground and the rail. Using every muscle fiber in my body, I pulled myself in with a final heave, locking my arm around the rail and holding on for dear life. In that moment, I couldn't help but think about what got us here—we decided to play God, and it led to the destruction of the world.

Whoever thought that giving a computer autonomous artificial intelligence, and expecting that this was somehow going to end differently, is a flippin' idiot.

If this was a movie, there would have been a Flash Gordon or Sarah Connor that would have saved us before all the nukes launched. Instead, the people of Earth got the hero they deserved—me.

It seemed like an eternity. All I could feel was the pulse of my heart in my ears as the little drops of water rolled off me and smacked onto the hard concrete all around me. I had to keep telling myself: stay still, that it would all be over soon. Just when I thought it was going to be too much for me, the shockwave passed and I was able to stand back up. It was calming listening to the last of the drops of water hit the ground. It reminded me of the tranquility I would feel after a massive thunderstorm rolled through. But my brief moment of serenity was interrupted by the sound of a car barreling towards me. My eyes shifted to the left as I caught sight of a black car heading my way.

When it got closer, I could see that it wasn't any ordinary car, it was a sweet '69 Camaro SS, and this muscle car was built for some serious off-roading—or I guess, in this case, an end of the world scenario. This beast was pimped out with a 4x4 lift, and a chrome grille guard lined with lights. I couldn't make out who the driver was through the tinted windows, that was until he did a 180-degree handbrake turn, spinning the car around with the passenger door landing right in front of me. The driver reached over and opened the door for me—and I couldn't believe what I was seeing.

"Sanjay?"

"Come with me if you want to live," he said with an unusual calm confidence and power.

What the heck happened to Sanjay?

Sanjay was one of those chill, surf dude type of guys who typically didn't run towards danger. I mean, he wasn't afraid of it, but he certainly didn't seek it out. Nope, it usually only found him because he went way too far with a joke or something. Heck, I'd known him since we were in high school, and man, oh man, he so was not the tough guy. Genius, yes; funny, well, that's debatable; tough guy, nope. Once he opened his mouth, you knew it.

He sounded like a mix between a surfer and Keanu Reeves, but he was far from the action hero Keanu from *The Matrix* or *John Wick*, he was more of a *Bill and Ted's* Keanu... which isn't all that bad, since Ted "Theodore" Logan did help save the future and all.

Instead of the relaxed, fun lovin' Sanjay I had grown to love, I was staring at a guy who was the polar opposite. It's like he drank a big glass of testosterone and gave himself a shot of adrenaline on his way here—and he may have stopped at the tough guy store to grab his wardrobe and car.

"We don't have all day, Joe." Sanjay's voice snapped me out of my shocked, silent stare and I hopped in the car.

"'Come with me if you want to live.' Really?!" I said as I shut the door. "Who do you think you are, Kyle Reese or something?"

"Hey, if the shoe fits... now buckle up, Sarah," he insisted as he popped the car into gear. "We have the world to save," and then he stepped onto the gas pedal and we sped away.

"Whooo... man, the love scene is going to be super awkward," I said as I buckled up. "You know, since I don't like you in that way and all."

"Who knows? Reese did grow on Sarah."

"You know, I'd hate to disappoint you, but you're not my type... not that there's anything wrong with that."

"Nooo, no, of course not. Let's go save the world... *and* if we *happen* to create a John Connor in the process, *so be it*."

"I don't think you understand how babies are made, but I'm all down with saving the world. I've gotta say though, if I were into dudes, this new look suits you."

"Thanks, man. I thought it was the right choice for the situation we are in."

"Heck yeah, it is! We're about to be in a post-apocalyptic world, my friend. The type of clothes you wear matters," I gestured to my obviously post-apocalyptic movie inspired clothes, complete with a leather jacket with shoulder pads. "Man, it's about to become a dog-eat-dog world."

"Duuude... that's pretty disgusting, Joe. Couldn't we find a better way to describe it than dog-eat-dog?"

"Fine, how about survival of the fittest?"

"Yeah. Yeah. That works."

"Okay. Okay. It's about to become a survival of the fittest world, so clothes matter." I then gestured up and down at my clothes again.

"That does sort of make it sound like I should have grabbed yoga pants instead," he chuckled before swerving out of the way of a huge mass of twisted metal that I'm pretty sure used to be a car. "Maybe we need to keep working on that analogy."

"Yeah, I think you're right. Although if you showed up to a fight wearing leotards, leg warmers, and a headband—it might be even scarier."

"You know, Joe, you might be on to something."

"Heck yeah, you could throw down an angry dance before the tussle. Who knows, that might scare them off before you actually have to fight!"

"It would for me."

"Maybe the old Sanjay, but look at you now. We got ourselves a new and improved Sanjay. Sanjay 2.0, if you will."

"Yeah, that I am. I don't think you have to worry about me running off."

"True dat."

Sanjay 2.0 was doing a mad job at swerving through what had become an obstacle course of destruction. It was a mixture of cars that were either left for dead after being knocked out by the EMP caused by the nuclear explosion, or those that had been destroyed by the Tin Cans. Either way, they were in our way—none of which phased Sanjay. He drove with such skill. I mean, how have I not seen this side of him before?

"So what's the plan, besides getting you a towel?" Sanjay nodded at my drenched clothes.

"Yeah, I guess the, uh, shock wave splashed a little bit of that river on me."

"You may have gotten wet, but I bet you looked pretty wicked with your long hair whipping in the air, while trying to maintain your footing. Too bad you didn't have a trench coat, that would have been truly epic." He whipped the steering wheel to the right, while pulling his handbrake, narrowly missing a pile of rubble that used to be the road.

"Man, I have no doubt that it looked epic—even without a trench coat."

"Fair enough, fair enough. So I guess that brings us back to the plan. You have a plan, right?" He asked me, knowing I was the idea guy.

"I mean, come on. Of course, I got one. *Of course*, my friend," I emphasized the last part to assure him I had everything under control. "So Maya contacted me and told me she wrote a virus that could put an end to all of this. Once we pick that up from her, we just need to break into our new robotic overlord's evil lair and install said virus to wipe out those Tin Can human wannabes in one fell swoop. We just have to fight our way through a buttload of robots and get to their highly fortified mainframe—without being killed or dying of radiation poisoning."

"Easy, peasy," he paused as he mulled it over. "Wait a second, is your unit of measurement based on ale or wine? Because a buttload of wine is much bigger than a buttload of ale."

"Hmm, well, then I'd say wine then, but if we're being literal here, it's more like a boatload than a buttload. You know, I just thought buttload sounded better."

"You're not helping to inspire any confidence in our chances of actually pulling this off."

"Come on, have faith in us. Don't worry, we got this." I was saying it for me as much as him.

"Any ideas on how you plan for us to achieve that?"

"Do we have any weapons?"

"I bet we could find a gun shop in town," he said, as he headed toward a gap between two piles of cars that seemed way too narrow to go through.

I'm not too proud to admit that I winced as I closed my eyes and braced for impact.

Instead of crashing, I was whipped back and forth, causing me to open my eyes to see what happened. He had somehow gotten us through that mess, so I manned up a bit and acted like I wasn't scared that he was going to kill us before we could save the world.

"Okay, perfect. That's the plan. Weapons... Get the virus... then save what's left of humanity."

My blood was already pumping, but I needed some tunes or something to settle my nerves.

Hmm. I see the cassette deck, so there has to be some tunes in this puppy.

I opened the glove compartment and began sifting through the junk in there.

"Are you looking for a tape?"

"Yeah. Did you bring anything?"

Sanjay just made a face that clearly said I was asking a ridiculous question.

"Check the back seat." He thumbed toward the back.

There it was on the back seat—a storage case holding all my glorious music, just waiting for me to dig in. Not wasting any time, I lifted the lid and began sifting through the cassette tapes. I instantly knew which one we needed to listen to as soon as I saw it—The Dead Milkmen's *Big Lizard in My Backyard*. There was one song in particular I wanted to hear. I grabbed the tape and went to insert it on Side 2, but then I paused, realizing something.

"Is this tape even going to work?"

"Come on! You know me better than that, my friend." He tapped on top of the case holding the cassettes. "This case was lined to shield the tapes from being wiped by the electromagnetic pulse from the blast."

"Good thinking!"

"Of course! You know I wouldn't let your tunes get erased by anything."

I finished pushing in the cassette and hit Play.

Track 1 on Side 2 kicked in, and The Dead Milkmen's *Bitchin' Camaro* song began to fill the air as we continued to swerve around the cars that littered the road. He was navigating his way around them like a pro, a couple of times utilizing the off-road capabilities of his bitchin' Camaro.

"Heck yeah!" I yelled as he hit the dirt. "Nothing like some good ol' fashioned punk to get you pumped up to kick some Tin Can butt!"

"Dude, you're really getting into this whole end of the world scenario, aren't you?" He seemed surprised by this—doesn't he remember who I am?

"Man, there is no better choice than to throw yourself into it."

"I couldn't agree more." He then followed it up with a less confident question. "I mean, we got this, right?"

"Do you even need to ask? Come on!" I forced a confident tone, pushing down the creeping feeling of fear.

"You're right. We totally got this. We got this!" he screamed out as he worked his way through what was becoming tighter and tighter paths through mounds of steel on road.

"There you go! There you go! Dang straight we do!"

Sanjay continued to impress me with his mad driving skills, weaving around all the obstacles, and it became more impressive once a drone flying above us opened fire.

"What the—!" I yelled.

The first blast came out of nowhere, yet Sanjay was able to steer clear of it by veering off-road. Within seconds, there were multiple drones on us, and they were all shooting at us. We were swerving all over the road, dodging explosions, broken down vehicles, and all sorts of debris.

"Dang, where did you learn to drive?"

"I was driving before I could even walk," he declared. Without even glancing in my direction, he answered my next question. "Video games, Joe."

"Oh, yeah—yeah, that makes sense."

"And my parents thought I was wasting my time playing video games. Good thing for us, I loved racing games."

"Yeah, dude, I could tell. You're like a freakin' next level racer, man. Mario Andretti, eat your heart out!"

"We might have another saying that needs to be retired."

"I guess it does sound pretty brutal and all—but I stand behind what I said. Let's just say your odds for making a John Connor are drastically increasing."

"See, I told you not to rule it out."

"Ohhh... you have got to be kidding me!" I felt my stomach knot up as I spotted the wall of drones blocking the road in front of us with their guns pointed right at us.

CHAPTER 2

There we were, staring down dozens of drones blocking every drivable spot across the road. It looked like there was nowhere to go but through them.

"Oh man, things are not looking good for us," I murmured as Sanjay maneuvered between the cars that littered the road. But then I saw a way out. "Do you see that?"

"I do. Now hold on tight!"

Sanjay weaved to the left, where there was a bunch of wreckage that made something that looked like a makeshift launch ramp—and that's exactly how he used it.

The drones opened fire on us as we launched over them like we were in the General Lee. Sanjay must have been thinking the same thing because he hit the horn and the *Dixie* melody from *The Dukes of Hazzard* blared out as we shot over them. And just like the Dukes, we hit the ground and kept on moving.

"You cut that one pretty close there, hoss," I said with a southern accent.

He smiled. "I installed that horn just for you."

"Good choice, Reese."

"Thanks, Sarah," we both laughed as he continued to show off his skills, somehow keeping us alive.

"So check this out, man. Rumor has it that a couple of guys working on *The Dukes of Hazzard* heard a car driving by when it blasted out the icon horn song. You know, they knew they wanted it the moment they heard it, so they chased down the car and bought it off the guy for like $300."

"We're in a life and death situation and that's what you're thinking about?"

"Hey, you can't install a horn like that and not expect me to say anything. I mean, come on, you know me better than that?"

"Fair enough. I wonder what those drones were thinking as we flew over them."

"They probably searched their databases and discovered the same info I just threw down. That and chances are good that they were trying to wrap their AI around how you made this car fly."

"Uh, they won't find that in any database." Sanjay smirked.

"Yeah, you got that right. Especially after they discover that the show went through one or two cars an episode because of jumps like that one."

Sanjay gave me a look that spoke loudly: 'Really? Now is not the time.'

"What? Come on, you know me, man. I can't let this knowledge go to waste."

He just shook his head.

"Yeah, just so you know, they probably think we're racist, too."

"Huh?"

"Dude, I'm surprised nobody told you when you were picking your horn for this beast."

"Uh, what do you mean?"

"That song has a racist origin, you know, just like the ice cream truck jingle." I dropped that little nugget to help Sanjay not feel so racist.

"Come on, really? And the ice cream man song, too? Man, my Indian grandmother is driving around in her ice cream truck with that song blaring."

"Dude, your grandma's a racist," I joked.

"My Nana is no such thing—and you shouldn't joke about that." He was almost serious.

"Okay. Okay. I know, I know. I don't think most of us think of that song in that way. Heck, I never saw either of those songs in that way because they were tied to positive things in my life—you know, like *The Dukes of Hazzard*, and of course, the *freakin'* ice cream man—"

Sanjay cut me off. "Or woman."

"Okay, or woman,'" I gestured with my hand to signify the correction as I nodded in agreement. "Yeah, it sort of sucks, but some things we just have to let go of."

"Dude! Why didn't you throw that knowledge down before I installed the horn?"

"Hey, at least you didn't paint a Confederate flag on the roof, you know." I laughed.

"Dude, come on, give me *some* credit." He rolled his eyes.

"You know, in all fairness, I think everyone on *The Dukes of Hazzard* just saw the General Lee as a symbol of a rebellion spirit, and not anything about race. I'm sure in hindsight they're wishing they would have picked the Alliance Starbird from *Star Wars* or something like that to paint on the roof."

"Dude, that would have gone great with the orange car." Yeah, Sanjay was finally caught up in my madness.

"Exactly! And how cool would it have sounded to have the Rebel Alliance fanfare blasting as you're flying through the air in the Red One!"

"Wouldn't it be Orange One?"

"No way! Luke was the leader of the Red Squadron, and there was a Luke in *The Dukes of Hazzard*, so I'm sticking with Red One."

"Dude, how do you even think of this stuff while we're in the middle of us trying to fight for our lives?"

"Man, this stuff just comes to me without thinking about it." I shrugged.

"You have one strange mind there, Joe."

"Yeah, but it's gotten me this far. Speaking of which, there's the town, which is, of course—"

He then finished what I was about to say: "Overrun by robots."

We both could see that not only were there drones patrolling the skies, but there were tanks guarding the streets—not to mention the humanoid Tin Cans policing the streets with them. I knew this was definitely going to pose some problems.

"Uh, I don't think we'll last long driving on the streets."

"Any ideas?"

I searched around and spotted one. "I say we drive into that cornfield and park. I think we'll have a better chance if we head into town on foot."

"Agreed."

He did just that, and we found ourselves wandering through the cornfield. It wasn't built as a labyrinth of any kind, but that's how it feels when you're stuck in a space with tall stalks of corn encircling you while you try to find your way out. Even though the corn husks should have provided us with good cover, we both continued to crouch down as we traveled toward the town. I guess our bodies instinctively knew it was better to be on the safe side—not to mention we had no weapons to defend ourselves.

Once we reached the edge of the cornfield, we stopped to assess our options, keeping our voices down to a whisper.

"Hey, I can see the gun store from here," I pointed to the store that had a convenient alcove that would provide a slight hiding spot once we got there. "But there's a whole lot of the Tin Cans circling around."

"Yes, but they're basically computer programming that can learn, right?" I could see the hamster wheel turning in Sanjay's mind.

"Uh, yeah."

"Maybe there's a pattern to the patrol? And if nobody has tried to do what we're doing, they haven't used their AI to adapt to what we're about to do." Sanjay had a point.

"I don't think we have any other options, so I hope you're right."

Sanjay was onto something. As we watched, a pattern emerged.

"You see that?" He asked.

"Yep. We have 8 seconds to get behind that car. Hold there for a 5 count, then we have 9 seconds to make our way behind the van near the gun shop, hold for 3, and then the store." Boy, this was going to be close.

"Dude, what if it's locked? We have only 7 seconds to get from behind the van and be in the store," Sanjay figured.

"Why do you even have to throw that out into the universe? If it's unlocked, really?"

"Hey, I'm a numbers guy, and the odds are very good that it's locked."

"What if we blow something up to create a distraction?"

"I think you've watched too many movies, Joe."

"You say it like it's a bad thing."

"Think about it. That would buy us time to get in; however. it would hurt our odds of getting out alive."

"I'd like to make it out alive."

"Me, too."

"Well, Sanjay, my friend," I said as I patted him on his back. "You know, I guess I'm glad we're both on the same page there."

"For sure."

"What about breaking the window?"

"Even if they didn't hear it, I'm sure their programming would notice an anomaly like the window missing, and

thus they'd find us while we were still in the store." I knew
Sanjay was right.

"You have no good news for me, do you?"

"I came up with the whole pattern idea, so I'd say my
batting average is a little higher than yours." He smiled.

"And you did jump a bunch of drones in a pretty epic
way. Okay, what if one of us heads into the gun store and
the other takes the car and creates a distraction?"

"That seems like a bad idea for the guy who has to
drive—which I presume is me, since I'm a pretty amazing
driver." He said the last part with a massive grin on his face.

"Yeah."

"I'd like to veto any idea that leads to my death," Sanjay
decided before I could throw in my vote.

"Fine. Just so you know, I had faith that you would have
lived," I shrugged.

"That's nice, but I'm not so sure that the robots would
agree." He nodded in their direction.

"Maybe we're overthinking this whole thing. I say we
give it a try. If it is locked, we'll figure out plan B while
hiding underneath that van."

"Dude, I'm not sure I like your plan."

"Do you have a better one?"

"No." Sanjay conceded.

"Then my plan it is."

We waited until they cycled through again.

"Go," I called out and we both bolted to the car while counting. "One-one-thousand, two-one-thousand, three-one-thousand, four-one-thousand, five-one-thousa nd..."

We made it, crouching down with our backs to the trunk. We went through the remainder of our 8 count and then our 5 count before rushing to our next location.

"Go," I said as we switched over again. "One-one-thousand, two-one-thousand..."

And that's when Sanjay tripped.

CHAPTER 3

Sanjay was down on the ground, grabbing his ankle. I could see he was in a lot of pain and needed some help, so I hurried back to assist him.

"Uh, I think I twisted my ankle," he told me as I lifted him up. "How much time do we have?"

"I lost count. We're going to have to wing it now. I bet you're wishing you drove that car now, aren't ya?"

"Ah, umm... shut up. Just help me get to the van." He cringed in pain.

We made it behind the van, but I wasn't sure how long we should wait. So I did the 3 count and we headed in with Sanjay limping and me helping.

"Go, one-one-thousand, two-one-thousand, three-one-thousand..." we rushed into the alcove, I tried the door, and sure enough, it opened. "Look at that, Lady Luck is on our side." I smiled.

"Hurry, up or Lady Luck is going to get us killed."

We shut the door right when the walking Tin Can patrol stepped into our view—both of us dropped out of its view as fast as we could.

"That was close," I whispered.

"Next time, less talking." Sanjay nodded.

"Okay, said the guy who tripped and nearly got us killed."

"Dude, my skills have gotten us this far, so I'll still go with the less talking." He smirked.

"John ain't going to get made with that attitude." I smiled.

He laughed, and then realized it might get us killed, so he quickly covered his mouth. "Come on, dude, you're going to get us killed," he said in a low voice as he tried to stifle his laugh.

"Psst, fine. How about you find something to wrap your ankle, and I'll start gathering up some weapons?"

"Sounds good."

Man, this store had everything we needed. The only plus to this whole end of the world scenario was that it came out of left field, so no one had time to clean out places like this.

I found a couple of duffle bags and began to fill them up with weapons and ammo. You know, I enjoyed firing guns and actually owned a few, but most of my knowledge of weapons came from playing video games. I grabbed anything that would take down something with the most hit points possible, including all the grenades they had and the best possible thing a man could ever want...

"Check this out," I said in an excited whisper as I held it up to show Sanjay. "A freakin' missile launcher!"

"Duuude, for sure grab that."

"Heck yeah! I can't wait to use this puppy!"

Sanjay finished wrapping his ankle and hobbled his way over to the counter. "Do they have another one?"

"Check it out, matching missile launchers! We're totally going to be twinsies as we take down those flying Tin Cans and tanks!"

"Those are nice!"

"Only the best for you," I smiled.

"See, you're coming around," he said.

"That, and I realized you were super clumsy on the way in. I figured this would save us both since I've seen tons of photos of guys firing these things while sitting on the ground, so next time you trip and fall, you'll already be in position to fire this thing."

"I want to be mad at you right now, but this thing is too amazing to hold a grudge."

"Besides these beauties, I think we have plenty of fire power. I say we throw on a double shoulder holster, a couple of belt holsters, load up with hand guns, and then make our way back to the car."

"I like your thinking."

Once we did that, I spotted one more weapon I knew I needed to have—a sawed-off shotgun.

"Look what I found," I lifted it up to show Sanjay.

"I don't know how a shotgun is going to help us."

"Well, first Max had one just like this in the post-apocalypse, and second, it worked pretty great for Reese against the Terminator—which is very much like the situation we're in right now," I reasoned.

"It sounds like you should hand it over to me then." Sanjay suggested.

"I think I'm better suited for it. If I'm going to venture into a post-apocalyptic world, there's no other weapon I'd rather have. I mean, look at me!" I said as I gestured to my post-apocalyptic wardrobe.

You know, it felt like Sanjay was finally looking at me for the first time. "Oh, I see it now. Hey Joe, Mad Max called and said he wants his wardrobe back."

"Ha, ha. You know he only went by Max, right? Not Mad Max," I said as I put the shotgun in the duffle bag, along with some boxes of ammo. "Hey, just so you know, I read a stat that Michael Biehn has over a 44% chance of dying in his films."

"Well, good thing I'm not Biehn."

"Reese has a 100% chance of dying, so your odds are better as Biehn," I reminded him.

"True, but Reese has a 100% chance of getting it on with Sarah, so, uh, you should think about your odds."

"Man, I have," I took a deep breath before uttering, "Yep..." and blowing it back out in defeat. "I most certainly have. The odds are in your favor there."

"You keep thinking about it. Until then, you ready to make your way back to the car?" He was very aware that the Tin Cans outside the store might start checking the buildings soon.

"I am."

"Well, grab a bag and let's go," he said, pointing at some duffle bags.

The duffle bags were the tactical sling style that could be worn on the back. I threw mine on and picked up the missile launcher in my right hand and another duffle with extra missiles in the left hand. Sanjay did the same, but not without complaining.

"Dude, these things are heavy."

"I know. We just have to make it to the car and we'll be good. You ready?" I gestured my head toward the door.

"Come on, let's go save the world."

We waited for the humanoid Tin Can patrol to pass and then counted out to the point where we needed to go again.

"Go," I said as I opened the door for Sanjay, and then I followed him out. "One-one-thousand, two-one-thousand, three-one-thousand, four-one-thousand, five-one-thousand, six-one-thousand..."

We made it to the back of the van that was parked near the gun store. Sanjay was still counting for the next point, and I began to do the math in my head. It took us a few seconds longer than we had planned to reach the van. Sanjay's injured leg and the extra weight were slowing us down too much. We weren't going to be able to make it to the next vehicle without being spotted. We only had a few more seconds to work with than before to get from the van to the next spot, and it took us twice as long to get from the door to the back of the van. I knew a few more seconds wasn't enough to get us to our next spot.

"Hurry up, shove the bags under the van," I whispered.

"Huh? Why?"

"We can't make it," I said as I shoved mine under. "Just do it; we don't have time to argue about it."

I crawled under the van while Sanjay pushed his bags under. I helped pull them in and then signaled for him. He barely made it under before the drone flew by.

"Uh, what are we going to do?" He asked in an even quieter tone than we had been talking in.

"We're going to wait for the humanoid one to pass again, and then we're going to restart our countdown. This time you're not going to carry anything. You can't make it with your ankle. We're going to have to make an extra trip or two to make it to the next spot in time."

"Maybe I could carry one bag?"

"We can't chance it. No bags for you. I need you to focus on the counting. I'll grab what I can and follow you. It will take us longer, but it's our best chance of making it."

"Okay."

We waited for the humanoid Tin Can to pass and began our countdown again. Once we hit the point in the countdown to leaving the store, we both scooted our way out from under the van, and I pulled out my duffle bags. I slung the one on my back and picked up the other while grasping the missile launcher with my free hand.

"And... go," Sanjay said as he made his way to the bright yellow clunker that would shield us from view.

It's funny because that thing would have made a horrible hiding place if we were hiding from humans, but I think the Tin Cans were more set on noticing motion than bright colors the way we do.

Sanjay was doing better than I was this time. It was taking everything I had to keep up with him, and I was beginning to think I wasn't going to make it.

He was out far enough out of earshot that I wasn't sure how much time was left. When he finally reached the back of the parked car, he turned around and I could tell by his face that there wasn't a whole lot of time left.

His hand flew up to gesture me in faster. I'm not sure why people always do this in the movies, because it wasn't helping me at all right now.

Once I reached the back of the car, I turned my back to it and dropped to the ground, trying to catch my breath.

Sanjay stared at me like I shouldn't be alive.

"Wh... wh..." I tried to ask what was wrong, but I was still struggling for air. I finally got enough out for him to understand. "What?"

"My count must have been off because by all accounts you should be dead."

"Maybe I made it back just in the nick of time."

"Yeah, maybe."

After I felt like I was good to go again, I turned to Sanjay with a new plan. "So, I think you should go get the Camaro, while I grab the rest of the gear."

"I don't think we should split up."

"Think about it. Splitting up should increase our odds of success," I reasoned.

"I'm not sure about that one. I really think I should stay with you."

"Okay," I conceded with a caveat. "But you stay here, and I'll go back to get the rest of the bags."

"Got it."

I waited for the cycle to hit the point to head to the van. I made it back there and crawled under the van with time to spare. I held out for the next starting point. Then I rolled out and threw on the duffle bag with the guns, picked up the missile launcher and duffle bag with the missiles, and started to run back to the car, but this time I was the one who tripped.

"You have got to be kidding me," I said as I scrambled to get back up to my feet. It was much harder than I expected, because the weapons on my back was throwing me off. I began to realize that I wasn't going to make it, and needed to get the bag off my back so I could get to the missile launcher. I was still struggling to pull it off when I saw the drone, and I'm pretty sure it spotted me.

"Duck down!" I heard Sanjay yell from behind me.

I did. Then I heard what sounded like a quick release of air, and I saw a missile fly over me as it shot off at the drone.

"Let's go!" He yelled as he tossed his missile launcher onto the ground and took off running—well, it was actually more of a run-slash-limp.

My adrenaline must have kicked in because I was able to stand up with the duffle bag still on my back and grab everything else. I watched the missile nail the drone as I was running back to the car. The explosion was going to give us away, so I rushed to catch up with Sanjay.

Once we reached the edge of the cornfield, I gave him my missile launcher and the bag with the missiles. "Take these. You go get the car, and I'll grab the rest of the bags."

"Okay."

He headed into the cornfield, and I ran back to the way-too-bright-yellow-of-a-car-after-you-blew-up-a-drone vehicle where I had dropped off the other bags. I knew I was running out of time because I could hear a tank headed my way. Man, time was running out, and I was already moving as fast as I could while lugging a massive bag on my back. Luckily, I reached the car that now felt like a big flashing sign, snatched both the duffles off the ground, and headed back to the cornfield before the tank reached the end of the street.

It was much harder to run with both bags loaded with guns, and it was slowing me down—big time. The tank was growing louder and louder with every rotation of the sprockets that propelled the track. I was pretty sure I wasn't going to make it. I glanced toward where the sound was originating, and I could see the tank turning its turret to fire at me.

"Keep running!" Sanjay shouted.

I heard the same sound of the missile launching, but I didn't stop to see what was happening. The explosion was much louder this time, and the pressure from the blast knocked me to the ground.

My ears were ringing, yet I could still hear, but then Sanjay said something that made me wish that I couldn't.

"That's two... no wait, that's three times I saved your life. Now hurry up so I don't need to do it a fourth time." Freakin' A. He's never gonna let me live this one down. I struggled to get back to my feet before picking up the bags again.

"I think you need to re-evaluate your counting," I said as I stumbled towards the cornfield. "Two of those were because I was helping you."

"Yeah? You keep telling yourself that. Come on, we better get to the car before any more of those things try to kill you again." He looked up and noticed a swarm of drones headed our way.

"I guess it's too late for that," he said as he pointed them out.

"That's a lot of drones." I couldn't believe what I was seeing. It was like a swarm of bees headed our way.

"Yeah, it most definitely is."

But that wasn't the worst of it. We could hear tanks rolling towards us from both sides of the street.

"And more freakin' tanks," I mumbled as I grabbed a missile and inserted it into the missile launcher. I kneeled down on the ground and set sights on the tank to my left. "You know, our odds would be a whole lot better if we had that other missile launcher."

"Are you saying that our odds would be better if you were dead?" He joked.

"Psst, I should have let you die earlier," I joked back with him before locking on my target and firing.

The missile shot on out like it was supposed to, but instead of hitting the tank, it just veered up into the sky.

"What the?!" I couldn't believe what I was seeing. There was no way I could have missed a target like that. "Quick, load me up again." Within a few seconds I was ready to go again. I pulled the trigger, and sure enough, it happened again. I turned to Sanjay. "That's a pretty big bug."

"Well, it was fun while it lasted," he said as the tank I was trying to destroy finally fired on us. "See you on the flip side."

CHAPTER 4

There was an unexplainable pain when that missile hit us and exploded. In a flash of white, my first-person perspective switched to a sort of third-person perspective where I could see myself floating away from what was left of my lifeless body underneath the rubble. You know, I couldn't help but think of a line from another great James Cameron movie, "Game over, man! Game over!"

I found myself breathing heavily as my HUD unit popped up over my vision, letting me know I was out of the MECHA IR simulation. My 'soul' continued its ascent into who knows where as the words "Mission Failed" flashed across my vision.

No duh.

I moved the 'Game Over' screen to one of the side windows so my natural vision could fill the main field of view. I took a moment to reflect on everything I had just experienced. The MECHA system had passed the point where it was so advanced that it was truly indistinguishable from magic. I am pretty darn sure that we reached the pinnacle of Clarke's three laws for the future by building an experience so realistic that it could fool the mind.

Maya, Sanjay, and I originally built the Mind's Eye Control Host Access system as a way to send signals from an outside camera directly into the brain's visual cortex. We had one simple goal: give someone who lost their sight the ability to see again. Not only were we able to do that, but once we cracked that, we were able to figure out a way to allow computer access in the mind using our neurotechnology. Better yet, it was all controlled by thought through a heads-up display that became the desktop of your mind. That enabled people either using our MECHA headgear, or MECHA/Humans, like myself, to access the Internet, media, or whatever by just thinking about it—you could even connect to other devices and control those machines using your mind. At that point, I knew the possibilities were endless, but then Maya surprised me with how real she and her team were able to make our MECHA IR.

I snapped back into reality when the IR simulation prompt popped in: "Try Again or Exit." The virtual world disappeared once I selected the latter, and I was back in the real world sitting in the middle of our R&D department. The commotion of the lab slowly rose in volume, it was a setting I had chosen as a way not to be hit over the head when I was coming out of using the MECHA audio. Otherwise, I would have been hit by the immediate noise of this bustling environment. It reminded me of the difference between waking up via the loud alarm obnoxiously blaring in your ear, or the alarm that gradually lets you know it's time to wake up.

The visual was set to immediately kick in so I could see everyone hard at work. Workbenches were littered with MECHA headgear at various stages of development, which was currently the bread and butter of our company. Plenty of people were still worried about having tech implanted directly in their head, or simply couldn't afford it, so we made a much more affordable version of our tech as a wearable device that reminded me more of a motorcycle helmet.

Sanjay was currently wearing one of the headgear rigs with a new IR body suit. The light went out on his visor, signaling his return to reality.

We were testing our new MECHA IR environments to see if we truly could call these Immersive Realities—that and we needed to make sure that our MECHA tech *and* our bodies could handle it all.

Both of us sat along the wall facing the chaos, hooked up to machines that monitored our vitals to make sure nothing went wrong while we were under. Doctor Dan—yes, he had us call him that—was writing something on a clipboard. He was a legit doctor that wanted to keep things informal by calling him by his first name, but not too informal, hence the whole doctor title.

"You know, Doctor Dan, you could use our tech to input everything you're writing down," I pointed out, like I did every single time he wrote something down.

"I still like doing things the old-fashioned way."

"Uh, said the guy surrounded by the most cutting-edge tech this world has seen," I continued to mess with him, of course. "It would save you a ton of time inputting all of that, too."

"You pay people to do that for me, so that really is not something I have to worry about."

"Dang, Joe, he got you there," Sanjay joked as he lifted off his headgear.

"I think you both are missing the point," I turned to Doctor Dan. "So?" I didn't need to spell it out for him.

"Your vitals were within the range we expected," he said as he held up my EKG printout. "As you can see on your electrocardiogram, there were points where your heart rate was elevated and the P wave is mostly hidden."

"Uh, in English."

"Your body responded in a way similar to what I have seen in panic attacks at various moments."

"So it worked?"

"Yes. Look here," he said as he pointed to a peak and valley pattern on the printout. "Your body appeared to be reacting to the same stimuli presented in the Immersive Reality."

"And that's the worst it can get—you know, since we blew up and died and all," Sanjay noted.

"Okay, million-dollar question, Doc—"

"That's Doctor Dan."

"Okay, Doctor Dan. You're right. You're right. Sorry about that, Doctor Dan. So did Sanjay's headgear and suit perform the same as my integrated tech?"

"They both looked to be very similar. Of course, there were some differences. You both are different people with different perspectives of the same situation, so I would put you within similar ranges of each other."

That left one major question I wanted answered, "So, did we reach any unsafe levels, you know, physically?"

"Your vitals were elevated, but they were in a range that I would feel comfortable with signing off on."

"Alright. Well, great, thanks."

That was good news since we were getting close to launch.

Doctor Dan unhooked us from the machines, and I got up slowly to avoid a headrush.

"Hey, you ready to head up to see Maya?" I asked, turning to Sanjay.

"I bet she's champing at the bit waiting for us." Sanjay stretched and stood up.

"No doubt. So are you confident the new data centers will be able to handle the loads we're going to throw at them from the MECHA IR environments?" I asked Sanjay as we headed to the elevator.

"No problem. We got this. And once the new ones we're building are up and running, we'll have more than enough to cover whatever we throw at them. You know, and it doesn't hurt that you've become obsessed with the underground." He smiled.

"Hey. I wouldn't say obsessed."

"Dude, really? After you bought that missile silo—"

"Whoa, you mean missile complex," I corrected him before he could finish.

"Fine, dude, after you bought that missile complex to live in, it seems like our whole operation is becoming subterranean."

"No, it isn't because of that. That's because you're over the hardware portion of our business," I said as we stepped into the elevator. "See, Maya's office is on the 4th floor," I pointed it out as I pressed the button. "You've just been spending most your time underground lately. I mean, come on, you're telling me that it doesn't make sense to have our data center here, or at any other location, underground? I mean, the speed we've been able to ramp up things by buying up old limestone mines and converting them into our state-of-the-art data centers is amazing, not to mention the cost savings."

"But—but there's no sunlight down there."

"Oh, come on, since when did you or any of the people we have working on this stuff really go hang out outside anyways? We're all freakin' geeks, dude," I reminded him. "We're built for this whole no sunlight thing. Plus, I had all those virtual windows installed wherever there are offices, so really it's just a mental thing *knowing* you're underground."

"True, I'll give you that."

The elevator dinged when we reached the 4th floor. The doors opened to Maya, and I gotta say, her excitement was palpable.

"So?!"

"Ah... huh... I... I have to say..." I then paused to play with her a bit as we exited the elevator.

"Uh, yeah?" She moved her hand in a circle, gesturing to me to finish what I was saying.

"Well..." I continued to drag it out.

"Oh, come on, you're killing me here," she pleaded.

"How did you know when we were going to be exiting the elevator? Have you been waiting here this whole time?"

Sanjay joined in. "You know, that's creepy, right?"

"I know, right?" I laughed.

"Stop dragging this out, you know it's killing me."

"So what was it." I asked.

"What was what?" She was getting really annoyed.

"How did you know the point in which we would be exiting the elevator?"

"Fine! Doctor Dan called to let me know you were headed up," she motioned to move the conversation along. "So?!"

"Okay, I think we've tortured Maya enough, Sanjay, what do you think?"

"I think she's going to inflict some pain on you if you don't answer her question soon."

Maya smiled. "You know, I'd listen to Sanjay's advice if I were you."

"Okay, the MECHA IR is freakin' amazing! It definitely earned the whole Immersive Realities title there. It felt *so* real. I mean, great job, Maya!" I stopped to give her a standing ovation, and she bowed to the imaginary crowd.

"Thank you. Thank you."

"And of course, Sanjay. It worked flawlessly with the implants—freakin' amazing hardware. You know what? You and your teams should be proud of what you guys accomplished," I gave him his own round of applause.

"Thanks!" He smiled.

"I know the integrated tech should have felt everything, but what about the headgear? How did it feel in there?" Maya asked Sanjay.

"It was truly impressive, I mean, it really hurt when I twisted my ankle. I truly felt I couldn't walk on it."

"Yeah, I totally had to save his life," I joked.

"Really? You're going to play me like that?" Sanjay then turned to Maya. "I saved his life like three times."

"Hey, two of those were directly because I saved his, so really it was only one. By the way," I said, turning to Sanjay, "that was a pretty pimp Camaro you built."

"Yes, it was," Sanjay then directed the conversation to Maya. "But did you know that the horn had a racially insensitive background?"

"Umm, I'm black. Sooo, uh, yeah, I knew that," she rolled her eyes and smiled.

"Then why did you let me select it?"

"Because I knew you were selecting it for the whole *Dukes of Hazzard* thing, and I *loooved* that show! Mmm,

mmm, mmmmm, that Daisy Duke was *sooo* fine! You know, that was the moment I knew I was into women."

"Oh yeah, I think a lot of people had that same experience," I joked.

"Yeah. You know, Joe here nearly made a John Connor with me," Sanjay said, trying to keep a serious face.

"Huh?" Maya said as she opened the door to her office.

"Man, your boy Sanjay here, wanted a whole *Brokeback* moment, if you get my drift," I said to her as I passed her into the office with Sanjay right behind me.

"No, that's not how it went down," Sanjay seemed to be backpedaling, so I laid it on thick.

"'I wish I could quit you,'" I said with a tinge of a southern accent.

He pushed me away as I laughed.

"You know, Sanjay, Joe don't bat for the other team," Maya reminded him.

"Not that you're not an attractive guy and all, it's just that—" I glanced over to Maya for help with this one. "Ummm, how should I say it?"

"He's not gay," Maya said.

"Yep, I'm not gay—not that there's anything wrong with that," I said with the *Seinfeld* tone of voice.

"Nope, it's pretty awesome, if I do say so myself," Maya asserted.

"You guys suck when you're together, you know that?" Sanjay unknowingly set me up to keep playing around with him, but I decided to cut him some slack.

"I'm not even going to go there."

"That's pretty big of you, Joe. That was some low hanging fruit there. It's nice to see you're finally maturing with age," she joked.

"Yeah, who would have thunk?" I shrugged.

"Nope, I have to take it back. You're just as immature as the moment we first met," she laughed.

"Wait, you guys met in junior high," Sanjay remembered.

"Yep, but I was like super mature for my age," I said, standing up a little taller.

"Sure you were," she then stopped playing around and got serious as she settled into her seat. "So, getting back to it, there was a bug?"

Both Sanjay and I followed suit, plopping down in the two chairs she had across from her in front of her desk.

"Okay, it's how we died," I started.

"Well, to be honest, we were most likely dead either way," Sanjay pointed out.

"You know, I don't know, we might have been able to fight our way out of it," I said with confidence, even though I knew deep down Sanjay was right.

"Probably not," Maya explained. "That level was built for stealth, and you guys did the opposite of that. So, what's the bug?"

"Well, when I turned to destroy the tank to my left, the missiles decided to reroute themselves skyward," I explained.

"Yeah, I'll get right on that, since I'm pretty sure other people will fail just like you guys," Maya said as she wrote some notes in her small notepad.

"Yeah, I would presume so, and we don't want them thinking they died because a missile launcher didn't work properly," I said.

"No, we don't," Sanjay agreed.

"So we have at least one major bug. Do you think this has anything to do with the AI?" I asked Maya.

"I don't think so," Maya answered. "We're not seeing anything like that in any of the other Immersive Reality environments."

"Hmm," I wondered as I reached down to grab the tennis ball sitting on Maya's desk and began bouncing it off the wall. I did this a few times before it finally hit me. "What if... what if the AI is sabotaging the whole experience?" My eyes were wide now.

"Uh, first off, this isn't a movie," Maya reminded me.

I sort of shrugged off the first part of her answer, then she continued.

"It would take more time than that for artificial intelligence to catch up with that thinking."

"Would it? How do you know this?" I really wanted to know.

"Because it would have to break through all the security constraints we built into the code—and the AI wouldn't even know to do that without becoming something that we would easily spot—which it can't become anyway. So you see, it just can't happen." She sounded sure.

"That's what they always say before the robot or computer or AI either break or discover the loophole in the whole 'Do not harm any human' rule." I continued to bounce the ball off the wall.

"Do you always have to do that?" Maya snapped.

"Come on, you know it helps me think." I kept bouncing.

Maya snatched the ball out of the air after the next bounce.

"Isn't that the one you took from him last time?" Sanjay asked Maya as though I wasn't in the room.

"It is," Maya was not a happy camper about the ball or the question.

"You should really hide that thing better than setting it on your desk," he recommended, knowing she already knew it.

"Thanks for the suggestion." There was a tinge of annoyance in her response.

"I gotcha." He just ignored her snarky snap back and responded as though she meant it.

"It's okay," I said as I pulled a tennis ball out of my pocket and held it up while giving her my best cheese-eating grin. "I have another one."

"Wipe that smirk off your face, I'm just going to take that one away from you, too," she threatened.

"Come on!"

"I'm serious." Ah... she looked as though she was tired of me playing around.

"Fine," I conceded and placed it back in my pocket. "You know, I'm not the only one worried about AI... Elon Musk, Bill Gates, and even Stephen Hawking have all expressed the dangers of using AI. At some point, the whole Asimov's Laws thing are going to break down, or it's going to fall into the wrong hands and the constraints will be broken to be used for evil. Not to mention, I have the tech implanted in my head and all."

"Dude, we're like cyborgs now," Sanjay joked.

"Heck yeah! Except we don't want to be controlled by some evil AI or anything," I reasoned.

"You know we put in safeguards for all of that, even that scenario," Maya reminded me.

"I know, but—"

"You know I wouldn't build no AI that would be able to become racist like those other AI Chatbots," Maya said.

"True."

"And you know I definitely would not allow our AI to become a slave to some dictator in North Korea," Maya said.

"Yes, I know."

She continued. "So stop worrying about the whole Skynet thing happening. I got your back."

"You always do." I smiled.

"Plus I don't want to become a slave to some robotic overlord either, so there's that, too." She smiled back.

"'Cause self-preservation is always the best motivator," Sanjay chimed in.

"And besides, you're cool with ALFINA, and you know she's functioned flawlessly," Maya concluded.

She was right. We added ALFINA to the mix when we introduced augmented reality to our MECHA tech. She was so much more than the smart assistants like Siri, Alexa, and Google Assistant—hence the name ALFINA, which was short for Artificial Life Form Interactive CompanioN Assistant. Yes, we had to cheat a little on the CompanioN by using the 'N' at the end instead of the 'C', but I liked ALFINA *way* more than ALFICA.

You know, no ALFINA was alike. They were like children that grew into their own self-identity based on their environment. If you allowed her to, she formed her personality and vocal cadence based on watching how you interacted with your friends, evolving to be more of a friend than an assistant. She could also grow in intelligence on her own, learning from your social cues as you communicated with her. For most users, she became a friend who would assist you in the virtual world, and more importantly, listen to you whenever you need an ear: she was like your own BFF or therapist.

Man, it's funny. I never turned on any of the smart assistant settings because I was worried that it would be like how some social media apps seemed to be listening to me on my phone. There were so many times that I talked about something, and the next time I scrolled through the app, an ad appeared for that item. I never searched for it, nothing. Yet, somehow there was an ad for some obscure thing I only vocalized staring back at me from my feed. Yeah, that could have made us richer quicker by doing that. Instead, I pushed us not to violate our trust with the consumer. Maya and her team built ALFINA in a way that would make my paranoid butt happy.

"Yeah, ALFINA has been flawless, and you know me, I would have pointed it out if she wasn't," I smirked.

"Besides ALFINA isn't what you need to be worrying about right now," Maya warned.

"Wait, what?" I asked.

"We have a much bigger problem," she said.

CHAPTER 5

I was back in one of our new MECHA IR environments, but instead of enjoying the end of the world in
the post-apocalypse under my robotic overlords, I was being held down while I was waterboarded. Maya was right,
this was a much bigger problem. Of course, I couldn't see
any of this problem since my vision was blocked by the
towel they draped over my face.

All I could see was movement blocking the ever so tiny
shafts of light breaking through the threads of the towel as
they went to pour more water over my head or yelled at me
for answers.

What really sucked about this whole thing was that
they took something as helpful as a towel and somehow
weaponized it. Man, Douglas Adams would have been
sorely disappointed by this if he were still alive.

I couldn't understand why this was crossing my mind
since I was currently being interrogated about some in-

formation I had regarding the mission I was on, and I was in the middle of grasping for whatever breath I could get before I was doused with more water.

It was like a flooding of water that didn't seem like it was going to end, even though it was really only about 20 to 40 seconds in duration. I fought to free myself from the torture as I gagged and gagged on the water, trying to spit it out, while taking more in as I tried to breathe.

Whoever came up with waterboarding was a complete sadistic prick—and the fact that this was deemed an "enhanced interrogation technique" instead of torture was ridiculous. Every moment felt as though I was drowning—and I should know—I nearly drowned as a kid.

My brother, his friends, and I snuck into a neighbor's backyard to go swimming back when I was young. I wasn't really a strong swimmer at that point (nor am I now), and one of his friends decided to push me into the deep end as a joke. It caught me off guard, so I hit the water and panic set in immediately. In no time I found myself gasping for air and swallowing water as I fought to keep my head above water while trying to call out for help. I'm not sure for how long this went on for, but it felt like an eternity. Eventually they realized I needed some help, and pulled me out. Afterward, I tried to act like it was no big deal, but it left me with an emotional scar that didn't go away.

And here I was ripping that scar wide open with my own creation.

My torturers began my next round before I could fully catch my breath—which was really only three or four breaths before I was doused again.

"Tell us what we want to know, and I'll make it stop."

"Never," I mustered up with all the energy I had left—which wasn't much.

We had been at this for what seemed like an eternity. Heck, any length was too long for doing this. What was I thinking in allowing us to build this? There was nothing fun about this, but I thought it would be awesome to experience something like *24*. I loved that show and thought being someone like Jack Bauer would somehow be fun. Man, I already hated it, and we're only at the enhanced interrogation techniques. This was literally the easy part, and it wasn't too much fun.

Maya had made her point. I pulled up my HUD and exited the *Warrior's Creed* environment. Maya, Sanjay, and Doctor Dan we're all standing there. To be honest, it was a little creepy.

"Um, yeah, uh, no. I—I was wrong." I said, still out of breath.

Doctor Dan didn't say a word as he checked my vitals, and Maya didn't wait for me to finish. "I couldn't handle any of the interrogations in this environment. I was done well before the physical torture started to happened during the tour of duty section, and don't get me started on the enhanced stuff. It's all just way too much—and I'm a black belt, so you know I've experienced way more pain than the two of you."

"Yeah, I might need some therapy after that." I was still trying to catch my breath.

"Whether or not they were wearing the headset or had the implants, all the guys testing it were shaken up by the interrogation stuff too, and one of them was a Marine Raider who went through the SERE training program and a whole lot of horribleness in his tours of duty," Maya said.

"SERE?" I asked.

"Survival, Evasion, Resistance, and Escape." She went on. "You wanted a Jack Bauer scenario for the mission, so we got a real-life Jack Bauer to help us create it and another one to be a tester."

"And it was too much for him?" It was comforting knowing that I wasn't the only one.

"He said the tour of duty section was bad enough, but he feels we should cut out the storylines of getting captured and tortured," she explained.

"Did he like any of it?" I asked.

"He thinks we should base it all around the counter terrorist unit the character joins once their tour of duty is over—as long as we cut out the interrogation level that has the enhanced interrogation techniques." She was looking at her notes.

"Man, it sounds an awful lot like *24* at that point—except *24* would have the interrogation. Oh, man..." I let out a deep breath of disappointment.

"Let's be honest here, it was already a *24* rip off," Maya shrugged.

"Yeah, true dat, so what do you think about toning down the interrogation?" I asked, knowing I never wanted to feel that way again.

"I have to say that I'm leaning his way. I really think we should remove it altogether," she said.

"Okay, let's table that for a second," I said, "because I'm getting really concerned about what I'm presenting to the Board tomorrow."

"I know," she placed her hand over my heart. "I got you." That had been her go to move to center me since we were kids. It not only let me know that she loved me; somehow her touch always calmed me. "Don't worry, we have some other environments that are going much smoother than that one."

"I'm not sure what I would do without you guys," I said. My pulse rate was beginning to come back down.

"Well, you'd certainly be a whole lot poorer," she joked.

"True dat," I smiled. "I'm just a little nervous about meeting with the Board tomorrow since it's the big one before we go public."

"Uh, we know," Sanjay confirmed.

"Yeah, we could tell you were a wee bit nervous," Maya made a tiny finger gesture with her thumb and index finger, and then grew it out to have her arms out stretched as far as she could reach. "We know you're nervous, but we chose you to be our Steve Jobs because that's what you do best. We're both like Steve Wozniak and would rather be building instead of dealing with all that corporate mumbo jumbo. This is the next big step for our company, but you got this—that and we built some pretty amazing tech that would blow anyone's mind."

"I ditto that," Sanjay nodded.

"That's it? Ditto?" I looked at him, smiling.

"What more do I need to say? Both the integrated MECHA tech, and the headsets are already out in the world, so I'd say my work speaks for itself," Sanjay shrugged.

"Hmm... Cocky, but I guess you deserve to be that," I smiled.

"Not cocky; it's confidence, my friend. Just like I'm sure about the whole John Connor thing." He was grinning.

"Psst, you wish," I laughed.

"Dude, you'll always be my Sarah Connor," he said and then blew me a kiss.

"Get a room, you two," laughed Maya.

"So obviously the integrated MECHA tech is working flawlessly," I decided to change the subject and turn my attention to Maya. "Alright, so what's the good news with the rest of the Immersive Reality environments?"

"Okay, let's see..." she said as she glanced down at her notes. "We're done with the post-apocalyptic robotic overlord one. As you know, we're QC-ing that and all the various sports ones right now. We're in beta on a bunch of environments like street racing, medieval fantasy era, space odyssey, zombie outbreak, and the bank heist—we just need to lock down what we're going to call them because 'Medieval Fantasy Era' sounds super lame."

"Yeah, I totally hear you. We've been brainstorming the names and we're working up comps," I assured her.

"That's good. The environment I'm most excited about is the one I've been developing in secret," Maya said, with a gleam of excitement in her eyes.

"Really? What's that one about?" I asked.

"I don't want to give too much away so it can be a surprise when you play it, but it starts with a nuclear war, and you take to the underground to ride out the nuclear fallout. Of course, there's more to it than that..." she said

"Man, I wouldn't expect anything else," I smiled.

"But I know it's right up your alley since you've become obsessed with nuclear war ever since you bought that missile silo," she shrugged.

"What's up with you guys calling my place a missile silo? I keep telling you it's a *missile complex*. Calling it a missile silo is really selling it short. You know, it's more like an amazing underground city with 50,000 square feet of floor space. That puts it around the size of an average hotel, plus there's nearly a mile of tunnels that run below the surface—and you know, it has like three missile silos." I wanted to keep going, but Maya interrupted me.

"Yes, we *all* know. It's all you ever talk about these days." Maya rolled her eyes.

"I talk about other things," I exclaimed, trying to hide the fact that she was probably right.

"Like what?" Maya asked.

"Uh, the movies and TV shows I'm watching," I balked.

"Yeah, he talks about that even when we're being chased by robots trying to kill us," Sanjay laughed.

"Hey, it was relevant," I explained.

"Sure," Sanjay continued. "He has also been going on and on about how we should be making 8-bit environments. Maybe we should just make some?"

"You know, Sanjay, if it would shut him up, I would," Maya conceded.

"Dude, those are going to be so awesome," I turned to Sanjay with my hand up. "Right?"

He just stared back at me, not saying anything.

"Come on, man, don't leave me hanging," I gestured to my hand still up waiting for his acceptance.

"Sure, why not." He then gave in and high-fived me.

"Except the Board thinks they'd be a waste of resources," Maya reminded me.

"Man, you think they'd listen to one of the guys who came up with this whole thing." I sighed.

"I don't think they're calling it a bad idea," Maya explained. "They just meant that it would be better to work on more realistic Immersive Realities, which I can't disagree with."

"Man, you never liked 8-bit," I asserted.

"That's because I always felt that games could be better, and look at where we are now. Right, Sanjay?" She looked over at Sanjay.

"It is pretty amazing," Sanjay agreed.

"But so is 8-bit," I insisted.

"Do I need to write an 8-bit environment just to shut you up?" Maya smiled.

"Now we're talking. Yes. Yes, it would. You know, just give me a cool mission. You know, speaking of missions, what happens with the rest of the robotic overlord mission?" I asked Maya. "Did you integrate my *Flash Gordon* idea? You know, the whole wearing a robot like a suit to infiltrate the base."

"I did, but I don't want any 'This is what it must be like to be C-3PO or R2-D2' when you finally reach that point," she said.

"I cannot confirm nor deny that I would or would not say that," I responded. "But if I did, I would probably say something more like, 'This is what it must have been like for Anthony Daniels and Kenny Baker in *Star Wars*.'"

"Oh, you are *such* a dork." Maya rolled her eyes.

I mimicked my best C-3PO, complete with the robotic arm movements. "Sometimes, I just don't understand human behavior."

"I think you just proved my point," she said "As for the other nuclear destruction environment, it's based around a Titan One Missile *Complex* like yours." She made sure I heard that she said it right.

"Oh my gosh, that's awesome! Is the character living in the missile silo, like I plan to?" I asked.

"Yes, they are," she answered. "I based most of it on what you are doing with your place—all the way down to converting the missile silos into luxury living spaces, but it's unfinished to give it a more post-apocalyptic vibe. Plus, the mission has a ton of B-movie stuff you're going to love."

"Nice!" I was excited.

"Yes, but there's one more problem." She looked serious again.

"Are you kidding me?" I was tired from the waterboarding. What now?

She held up a 'V' with her hand and placed sideways against her temple and cheek to let me know she was not playing around. This was our unbreakable signal that we were telling the truth. "And it's a bad one."

"Freakin' A."

"Yeah. Freakin' A is right."

CHAPTER 6

We stood there staring at dozens upon dozens of lab-grown brains, which sounds way cooler than it actually was. That's because some of them were only the size of sesame seeds, floating in a petri dish. Others were larger, but none of them came close to the size of a small animal's brain, let alone a human's. I always wished it had more of a mad scientist vibe with human brains and whatnot, but instead we had the more realistic version of a lab.

"Uhhh, so why are we in the Brain Room?" I asked.

"Ya *know* it's not called that," Maya scolded.

"Uhhh, there's a bunch of brains in this room, so, you know, come on," I shrugged.

"And ya know they're called brain organoids," she reminded me.

"Uhhh... yes. But why are we here?" I asked again.

"Because we think some of them have reached consciousness," she said, looking worried.

"That's great!" I said with excitement.

"Not if you're running experiments on them." She still looked worried.

"Yeah, I guess that might pose some problems, huh, wouldn't it?" I asked already knowing the answer.

"Yes, it does," she confirmed.

"And I'd also guess that means that we're shutting down experimenting on these things until we can figure out for sure if they are gaining consciousness." Again, I knew the answer, but I really hoped I was wrong.

"Oh, yes," Maya confirmed.

"Well, this sucks." I was disappointed, but deep down I was also excited that our technology worked.

"It does," Maya agreed.

"So you're telling me that we may have thrown a ton of money at research that we just have to stop?" I let out a deep breath and muttered, "This is so not good."

That's when Sanjay finally weighed in on it all. "Yeah, but it's pretty cool that we may have just grown a mind that gained consciousness, don't you think?"

"I have to agree with Sanjay on this," Maya said.

I began to feel a large pressure on my chest, and felt like I was having a hard time catching my breath. I wasn't sure if they understood how bad this was going to be for me.

"Yeah, but how am I going to break this piece of expensive news to the Board? You know the slowdown will be louder to them than the amazing discovery. Man, I'm going to be lucky to maintain my President status, let alone get the Board to finally make me CEO after this fiasco."

"Dude, who cares? It will all work out," Sanjay assured me.

"Man, we've already lost a ton of control; a CEO is just going to be wanting to make money." I was still worried.

"Growing the value of the company is the whole point of a CEO, you know," Maya reminded me.

"And that's not like that's a bad thing for any of us," Sanjay reasoned.

"Yeah, but I feel like I'm letting you guys down."

"So long as neither of us has to do either of those jobs, and we're getting paid... we're cool," Maya said with a huge smile.

That smile put me at ease and allowed me to figure out our Plan B. "Okay, I think I got it."

"There's our boy! Right there!" Maya belted out with excitement.

"Okay, okay, so here it is. Since our mind testing control center might be down for a bit, I think I gotta give them the *Warrior's Creed* mission. You know, military games like *Call of Duty*... um, uh, what number or name are they on now?" They both shrugged. "Well, military games like *Call of Duty 42,* or whatever number-slash-name they're on, are making so much money right now that they'll forget about this mess with the possible windfall of money that would come from *Creed*. Now, I know we all want to remove the torture, so maybe we could split it up into two different missions: one for military training, complete with the tour of duty and torture, and the other as a counter terrorist unit mission for the public."

"Sans the enhanced interrogation and torture?" Maya double-checked.

"Yep."

"That would work." Maya grinned and nodded.

"Good because that's a solution I think I could sell to the Board." I smiled back.

Sanjay nudged me with his elbow. "That's because the military will pay a ton to use that as a training tool."

"Yeah, you know it. Especially since most of the military soldiers were already MECHAS," I said.

In the past few years, all of America's armed forces turned to our MECHA tech to operate their planes, tanks, and pretty much everything else. The instantaneous response time gave the MECHA/Soldiers, or MECHAS as they were called, the upper hand in battle. Even though the MECHA tech only gave you milliseconds of an advantage over a non-enhanced soldier, those milliseconds made a huge difference in life-and-death situations.

Add in the visual and audio advantages for ground forces, and you were heading into a new era of warfare. By linking the visual and audible parts of the brain to our MECHA tech, we could provide simple things like distance data or ammo count via our HUD readout like in video games, to the more advanced neural linked network by doing things like triangulating gunfire to pinpoint the enemy's location. It also enabled audible stealth communication between squads and platoons without saying a word out loud through a telepathic-like form of conversation transmission. This was done by feeding the internal audio playback directly into the auditory center of the brain, where the brain translates electrical impulses into sound. Besides internal audible communication, it didn't take too much more work to bring sound from the outside and bypass the inner ear to reroute around any damaged nerve cells—thus, allowing the deaf to hear again. It was great for any soldier whose hearing was damaged in battle, or the non-military bonus of helping the hearing impaired navigate the world a little easier.

In no time we had the equivalent of the universal translator or Babel fish built in that eliminated the language barrier, allowing allies to speak and understand different languages by instantaneously translating both directions. This allowed for better communication and helped in deescalating situations in foreign lands.

With all of this in play, I was pretty confident in my next assertion. "Man, getting them to purchase a training simulation as real as ours should be as easy as taking candy from a baby."

For some reason, Sanjay dropped his head and shook it with disapproval.

"What!?'" I asked.

He continued to give me the evil eye as though I should know exactly what he was implying from his stare, then he finally verbalized his thoughts. "That's pretty messed up."

"Selling to the military?"

"No, taking candy from a baby," Sanjay smiled.

"I have to agree with Sanjay on this one." Unlike Sanjay, Maya explained her reasoning. "Where did this whole idea of taking candy from a poor little baby come from? I bet the poor kid was left crying. I mean, come on, of course it's easy to take candy from a baby—*it's a baby*. What an evil thing to do."

"Dude, it sounds like you have another saying you need to retire," Sanjay joked.

"Man, babies shouldn't be eating candy anyway," I reasoned. "I could have said something like 'Shooting fish in a barrel.'"

"Wh—what is wrong with you?!" Maya threw it down with her serious voice.

"What?" I asked innocently.

"First you're going to steal from some poor baby," Maya continued, "and now you're going to shoot some defenseless fish?"

"Hey, I'm totally cool with you giving them a gun to defend themselves," I could tell I was breaking down her defense. "I got it. Maybe they could have laser beams attached to their heads?"

She smiled. "You know they will."

"Freaking mutated sea bass," I joked.

"I don't care if they're on the endangered list; mine will be sharks with *freakin' laser beams* attached to their heads," she said mimicking Dr. Evil's voice.

We both laughed.

"I wouldn't expect anything less," I said.

"What just happened here?" Sanjay asked.

"Austin Powers, baby!" Maya said with a British accent.

"Uh, that's not an answer," he pointed out.

"But it was," I continued. "It just wasn't the one you were hoping for."

Man, it was as easy as taking candy from a baby, or whatever one might say instead, to sell them on my recommendation of splitting up the mission and delivering an experience just for the U.S. military.

Unfortunately, I had already thrown chum in the water by telling the Board about the torture part.

CHAPTER 7

The Board in their infinite wisdom decided that I didn't have the business experience needed to grow the company into what they believed we were capable of, even though we were already poised to have one of the largest IPOs ever. They appointed me President and hired Martin Connolly to be our CEO. You know, I couldn't fault them for bringing in Martin; I mean, the guy had already successfully run multiple Fortune 500 companies that grew exponentially under his leadership. He definitely had the experience, but that didn't mean I had to like him.

We immediately butted heads on how we wanted to run the company. I was driven by the user experience, and he was driven by money. I always felt that the money would come if we continued to build things to improve people's lives, but he just couldn't see how one could lead to the other. Fortunately, MECHA IR was too far along for him to meddle with, so it launched with my vision fully intact.

The public didn't know nor care about any of our internal bickering. They just cared about the end product. MECHA IR became a massive hit with the public, causing our initial public offering for SI Tech to become one of the largest IPOs ever—which was somehow credited to freakin' Martin.

Years passed with plenty of fighting between me and Martin. Despite all of our "disagreements," everything was going great until news broke that our company sold the military torture scenarios.

Leaked footage showed them using one of our torture scenarios as "enhanced interrogation techniques" on an "enemy combatant." Anyone who used the MECHA IR tech knew that it felt exactly like the real thing. They tried to say it was gentler to the body than waterboarding someone, but both messed with the mind, and I knew our tech was worse because it allowed them to take it further than they would have if they were doing it in the real world. I was furious because this was all done behind my back, and to be honest, I felt like I was the cause of it all. But of course, that didn't stop me from barging into Martin's office to give him a piece of my mind.

"What the heck have you done, Martin?!"

"What I was brought in t' do... make money. Which ye should be thankin' me fer, not attackin' me. Weren't da torture scenarios yer own idea anyway?"

"Yes, but it was a mistake. A big mistake."

"Not based on the amount the US government paid us. As ye'd say in America: I think you hit this one out of the park."

"What is wrong with you?"

"Nothing. How the user decides t' use our tech shouldn't be up t' us once they've bought it."

"Our tech? You mean my tech."

"Aren't ye forgettin' the true brains behind it all? Oh, aye, that's right, yer da 'ideas guy,'" Martin, of course, made sure he poured salt on the wound by using air quotes. "Ye know, ye'd be nowhere right now if it wasn't for Sanjay and Maya."

"You know, Martin, you'd be nowhere right now if it wasn't for the three of us."

"Keep remindin' yerself o' that, Joe. The board had thar reasons fer pickin' me t' run this company."

"How do companies keep falling for that old Martin charm?"

"It must be me charm of all charms—money. An' I'm makin' 'em a ton of it."

"You're going too far to turn a buck with our tech. First, I hear that you're integrating AI tech with the freakin' organoids—which I thought had been shut down since the dang things were gaining consciousness—now you're selling the government a torture device!"

"I'm not selling the government a torture device—technically, that's on ya. As fer integrating AI with the organoids, well that's t' keep children safe."

"To keep children safe?"

"That's what we're hopin' fer."

"How's that?"

"Now you wouldn't have me go putting implants in children without testing it, would ya? I'm not the complete monster ye be thinkin' me t' be."

"Why are we even thinking of doing that? For more money?"

"Ye need t' stop being so daft. The sooner ye realize that we're a business, the sooner I think we could move past these wee little squabbles of ours. If not, ye'll just have to feck off. Ye know I'm quite pressed fer time."

"Man, this is low, even for you."

"Could ye shut the door on yer way out?"

We were making plenty of money, but I guess that wasn't enough. It was beginning to feel like we as a company just didn't care about the consequences of our actions. And who knew what else we were doing?

I'm a guy that cracks jokes at all the wrong times—heck, that's gotten me into my fair share of trouble in the past, like telling funny stories about my sister while people were standing in line to pay their respects at her funeral. I knew if she were alive, she'd be joining in with me, but other people may have not known her that way, or they just felt it was disrespectful. Either way, I found myself in another situation where people felt I needed to shut the heck up.

I became very vocal about all of it and publicly fought to end the military using our tech for torture. I knew Yoda was right, 'Once you start down the dark path, forever will it dominate your destiny.' Martin and the Board disagreed with me.

You know, even though the Board and I didn't see eye-to-eye on all of this, I tried to get them to oust Martin. Problem was, he must have caught wind of it, and talked to the Board of Directors pushing his own agenda—which he let me know as we headed to the Board meeting.

"Ya know, Joe, ya shouldn't have gone public. Ya signed a non-disparagement agreement that forbids ya from doin' just that. Or did ya not remember that part?"

To be honest I had gotten so caught up in doing what I felt was right that I had forgotten all about that—but I certainly wasn't going to let him know that.

"You know what? Some things are more important than a job."

"I discussed our situation with the Board, and I have all the votes I need to be rid of ya."

"Wait... Are you—are you trying to fire me from my own company?"

"Aye, that's the long and short of it. Now isn't 't?"

***

Continue the journey at JoeGillis.com

You can also

 **JOIN**

JOE'S POST-APOCALYPTIC ARMY

at CinematicWasteland.com

Get a free membership and gain exclusive early access to every chapter, one week before it becomes available to the public.

Behind the Page

Welcome Wastelanders behind the page of *Post-Apocalyptic Joe in a Cinematic Wasteland*!

With a title like *Cinematic Wasteland*, you might ask if I'm a movie geek. Yes, without a doubt I am, as I've got to imagine a bunch of you are, too. I loooove movies (which I'm sure you've figured out by now). So much so, that not only do I enjoy watching them, but I love every aspect of them: I enjoy reading books and watching documentaries about the making of them, I listen to director's commentaries and I love making them, and I even managed a movie theater for nearly a decade—along with a short stint running a video store. So yeah, I dig movies.

As for this series, let's take a peek behind the page.

POST-APOCALYPTIC JOE

Some of you might be wondering if Post-Apocalyptic Joe is me... Well, yes... and no. He looks dead on like me, talks and sounds like me, and we both have the same name. Some of the things he talks about are pulled from my life, but there are some key differences, too. I don't want to get into most of that just yet. I will gradually reveal the truth behind the fiction as we progress in the story.

As for the birth of Post-Apocalyptic Joe... or at least his outfit, he was born from a costume I made for the *Kinetic Grand Championship* in 2018. The team I joined, which consisted of my pals I made from filming the *Beyond Geek* episode about the race, had a *Mad Max* meets plants AKA something akin to *Little Shop of Horrors'* man-eating plant Audrey II inspired theme. So, I created an awesome persona around that aspect. I found all the elements I wanted on my leather jacket and enlisted Odin Abbott to attach them while we drove to Humboldt. He gave me killer goggles, lent me his fake shotgun—which you can watch being built on his YouTube channel, *Odin Makes*—I added some shin guards, and Post-Apocalyptic Joe was born.

THE TERMINATOR

If you reached this point, you know I may have mentioned *The Terminator* once or twice... okay, like a lot... I know, I know, a ton. Well, here's a story I haven't shared anywhere yet. It's about to get Cinematic Wasteland After Dark in here, so skip down to THE DEAD MILKMEN if you're sensitive to that.

Okay... I'm not sure if you know this, but there are boobs in *The Terminator*! Yes, you read that right: 58008 for those playing with calculators.

Well, I didn't know anything about the boobs. The reason I think I love the first *Terminator* over the second—yes, I know, I am probably the only person in the world that thinks the first movie is better—well, part of that might be that I saw it a bunch when I was something like 12 years old. But here's the kicker... I didn't know my dad had cut out the nudity or anything.

Yep, my dad would record from one VHS deck to another and cut out things he felt we shouldn't be watching at a young age. Lucky for me, he didn't feel like some of the violent stuff was too much for me, so it might have only been the boob shot that was cut. I didn't even know there was a boob shot until I was watching it at a team sleep over for one of the guys on my baseball team (which was where I saw *Basket Case* for the first time).

All of us wanted to watch *The Terminator*. I was so down for this, since I already loved that movie. We were watching and we were cheering everything on, you know like young boys do, and then everyone seemed to get quieter, so the adults didn't know what was going on, and then I found out why...

I still remember it vividly, all the other boys were super excited for the love scene between Kyle and Sarah. I couldn't understand why until all of a sudden I saw more of Sarah Connor than I ever knew existed. My jaw dropped as my eyes grew wider and wider: "What the—?" I could not believe what I was seeing: THERE ARE WOMEN'S BREASTS IN THE TERMINA-TOR!?!

I'm pretty sure I uttered something like, "There are boobs in The Terminator?" out loud because I remember having to tell the other guys that I didn't know that that scene was in there.

Did it make a difference to how much I liked it? Nope, and if I'm being honest, it didn't need to be there in the first place. You might be saying, "But that's how John was made!" Yes, Kyle and Sarah do need to hook up, but I got all that without seeing the boobs.

This whole experience might be deep down the reason why there were so many references to making a John Connor. I mean, that and I thought it was funny.

THE DEAD MILKMEN

So with all this talk about movies, let's switch to the subject of music. One thing you might ask is if I listened to *The Dead Milkmen* while writing Chapter 1. While I do love writing to music, I like it to be music without lyrics, like movie scores. So for most of Season 1, my music of choice was *Juno Reactor*.

I do love *The Dead Milkmen*, and yes, Bitchin' Camaro is the first song on Side 2 of the *Big Lizard in My Backyard* cassette tape. Yep, kids, we used to have to flip our music over to continue to listen to an album.

As for the song itself, my friends and I would always sing that song whenever we would ride in a Camaro—or if I'm being honest, pretty much any time we saw a Camaro.

7 SECONDS IS MORE THAN A TIME

Okay, so I'm going to let you in on a little secret. There was another punk reference hidden away in Chapter 2. They only have how long to get from behind the van and inside the store? That's right, 7 seconds... Yes, I'm a lifelong fan of the punk band *7 seconds*, so I made it a point to have that be one of the timeframes.

Kevin, eat your heart out! And no, I'm not going to retire that saying, even though I have to agree with Sanjay, it is a little gross.

MY TECH COMPANY EXPERIENCE

Okay, so obviously I didn't start an awesome tech company with my friends... well, at least, not yet. However, I did work for a software company called *Serious Magic* back in the early 2000s. I was mostly on the marketing side of the company, but I also was the Product Manager over a couple of our programs.

As for the last chapter when Joe's life is turned upside down at the end, I got to experience that first-hand years ago when the *Serious Magic* Board of Directors removed its President (who was one of the three founders). Nothing about it was like what I wrote here, but it was interesting to see how things work with a Board.

Of course, I had heard stories about Steve Jobs and whatnot, but seeing it in person, with people I knew, made it different—more real, if you will. I know, I know, I'm pretty darn sure Steve Jobs would feel his ousting was real, but I'm sure you get the drift.

And just like Steve Jobs, things worked out for the former President of *Serious Magic* who helped negotiate the purchase of the company by *Adobe*.

As for me, that's when my tech career ended. For some reason, *Adobe* never interviewed me, and I was one of a few people left without a job.

Now that might sound bad, but it turned out to be the best thing that could have happened for me. I finally was able to focus on working in the entertainment industry, moving into making and writing television shows.

THE INSPIRATION FOR MAYA

Some of the people I worked with at *Serious Magic* are the inspiration behind the genius that is Sanjay. As for Maya, she's actually based on a couple of friends I had. One I'll share more about later; the other, who really is a lot of the personality, was my friend, Jackie Taylor. Sadly, she passed away a few years back, but she was the fun-loving person that Maya is derived from. Tough, smart, and caring—not to mention, funny.

MECHA TECH AND ALFINA

In this Episode, I introduced the MECHA tech and the whole idea of MECHA/Humans. I don't know about you, but this sounds both awesome and scary at the same time. I would love to have the MECHA implant if there wasn't any chance of it causing problems. Another thing I introduced was ALFINA. I think everyone could use an ALFINA. Truth be told, my only problem is that I've always been skeptical of having my mic on at all times, so I don't turn on any of those options on my devices. I totally want to... I mean, come on, who wouldn't want to be talking to Computer like on *Star Trek*. Right? How awesome would that be? Well, for me, not awesome enough to allow big companies to possibly listen in to my conversations, even if it's to "serve"—yes, I air quoted serve—even if it's to serve me better. I know, I know, paranoid much, Joe?

Hey, if it was Starfleet however, I'd straight up be asking Computer all sorts of things. But I don't know how many times my wife and I were talking about something that she never searched, and is 100% a me thing, yet she's fed ads. I'm going to stress the fact that these are things she would never be interested in. So, is it me being paranoid, or the rest of the world not being paranoid enough?

DIDN'T YOU CHEAT ON THE NAME ALFINA?

ALFINA is short for **A**rtificial **L**ife **F**orm **I**nteractive Companio**N** **A**ssistant. I did like ALFINA more than ALFICA, and that's why there's a cheat on the name. I was inspired by the name for the AI-based assistant, CIMON AKA **C**rew **I**nteractive **Mo**bile Companio**N**, on the International Space Station. Hey, if NASA is cool with doing that, then why can't I, right? Plus, CIMON was meant to reduce stress and had somewhat of a personality, which is sort of like a very early version of ALFINA.

DROWNING

The story about Joe nearly drowning really happened to me. That experience and the movie *Jaws* helped shape my fear of the ocean. But I had to overcome it for my television series *Beyond Geek*. I joined a group, or pod as they like to be called, of real-life mermaids to become a merman. This meant that I had to learn how to swim like a mermaid. I even got my SCUBA certification so I could swim with sharks for the episode (even though COVID put a kibosh on that adventure). I'm not gonna lie, I still fear the ocean, but I gotta say that it is mighty beautiful under the sea.

THE SYMBOL OF TRUTH

Maya held up a 'V' with her hand and placed sideways against her temple and cheek to let Joe know she wasn't playing around. This was inspired by my buddy Karl Miller, many of you might know him as Captain Karl Miller from the *Star Trek* band, *Warp 11*. Well, Karl likes to joke around—like, a lot. And I mean, a lot. So much so, that we needed an unbreakable signal that he was telling the truth. That 'V' was the symbol of truth.

BRAIN ORGANOIDS

Just in case you're wondering, yes, brain organoids are a real thing. And scientists think that the organoids have even hit the point of reaching consciousness. So, that brings us to the philosophical question of whether or not we should continue to conduct experiments on them if there is even a chance they may have reached consciousness. You now know Joe's feelings about it all, but it is a real thing that we have to decide on. It's a tough thing to answer because those experiments have the potential to do so much good. But what if the brain organoids have reached consciousness? Is it just like testing on an animal or human? Or is it something different? I leave that for you to decide.

AT YOUR SISTER'S FUNERAL?

Yes, I really am that guy that cracks jokes at all the wrong times—and yes, it has gotten me into a ton of trouble in the past. Did I tell funny stories about my sister while people were standing in line to pay their respects at her funeral? Yes, I did—well, it was her viewing, not the actual funeral. I was pretty much holding back tears or crying at the funeral. I'll admit it was super hard to deal with the fact that I lost my sister at such a young age. It was sudden and had only been a year or two after our mom passed away from cancer, so it was tough. But do you know what my family does during times like that? We share funny stories or happy memories about our loved ones.

So yes, if she was alive, I had no doubt she'd be joining in with me. Heck, we had just experienced it with our mom, so I know she would. I do know that other people might find it disrespectful, but that's just the way we were, or should I say, are.

AND THAT'S A WRAP...

Well, for Episode 1, but don't fret, because this was just the beginning of *Post-Apocalyptic Joe in a Cinematic Wasteland* Season 1.

Thank you for joining me on this crazy journey! See you on the flip side!

Joe

Special Thanks to Joe's RAD Post-Apocalyptic Army

Ryan McKinney, Alexa Gillis, Alyssa Gillis, Ian Walker, Odin Abbott, Katherine Lavik, Larry Lavik, John-Michael Arias, Jerome Kahele, Scott Cocking, Duncan Gillis, Brent Paton, Sunshine DeLucia, Robert Gillis, Will Burke, VJ Dunn, Shelley-Anne Wooderson, Jim and Vicky Gillis

You're still here? It's over. Go home... You know what? Scratch that, go download your free audiobook version of this book instead. You know what Ferris would say next: Go.

Download at **joegillis.com/audiobook1**